S0-AHK-297

jellybeans

red marker— pg 14 11/2023

jellybeans

Sylvia van Ommen

Foreword by **Glenn Murray**
co-author of **Walter the Farting Dog**

NRC CASS COUNTY PUBLIC LIBRARY
400 E. MECHANIC
HARRISONVILLE, MO 64701

North Atlantic Books
Berkeley, California

0 0022 0413106 0

Copyright © 2002, 2006 by Sylvia van Ommen. English translation © 2004 by Nancy Forest-Flier. All rights reserved. No portion of this book, except for brief review, may be reproduced, stored in a retrieval system, or transmitted in any form or by any means—electronic, mechanical, photocopying, recording, or otherwise—without the written permission of the publisher. For information contact North Atlantic Books.

Published by
North Atlantic Books
P.O. Box 1232
Berkeley, California 94712

First published in the Netherlands by Lemniscaat in 2002
Printed in Canada

Jellybeans is sponsored by the Society for the Study of Native Arts and Sciences, a nonprofit educational corporation whose goals are to develop an educational and crosscultural perspective linking various scientific, social, and artistic fields; to nurture a holistic view of arts, sciences, humanities, and healing; and to publish and distribute literature on the relationship of mind, body, and nature.

Library of Congress Cataloging-in-Publication Data
Ommen, Sylvia van.
  [Drops. English]
  Jellybeans / by Sylvia van Ommen.
    p. cm.
  Summary: Two friends, a rabbit and a cat, speculate about what heaven will be like as they enjoy a visit to the park.
  ISBN-13: 978-1-55643-632-1
  ISBN-10: 1-55643-632-7
  [1. Heaven—Fiction. 2. Rabbits—Fiction. 3. Cats—Fiction. 4. Friendship—Fiction.] I. Title.
PZ7.O54855Je 2006
[E]—dc22
                                    2006023652

1 2 3 4 5 6 7 8 9 trans 12 11 10 09 08 07 06

Foreword

In the spring of 2005, I was speaking at a literacy festival in Albany, New York, and a well-known local bookseller, Frank Hodge, pulled me from the hubbub into a cloakroom and read aloud to me from *Jellybeans*. I was delighted. I was amazed. I was eager to get a copy right away. Since then, I've read this book all over North America and have frequently given it as a gift. In absolutely every instance, reading it produced a strange charm in the room. Now North Atlantic Books has brought out the paperback edition, and I am especially pleased to have an opportunity to say something here about this extraordinary little book.

As co-author of the *Walter the Farting Dog* series, I have always been interested in pushing the edge of the envelope. Books are not just something to be read, but should also serve to instigate a discussion, especially with children. Franz Kafka once said, "A book should serve as an axe for the frozen sea within us." *Walter the Farting Dog* tries to be such an "axe," raising issues such as taboos, tolerance, the fallibility of parents, acceptance, and other subjects that children need to hear about and discuss. *Jellybeans* is cast in the same mold, and here we have a cat and a rabbit—with cell phones, adept at text-messaging—leading us oh-so-simply into the very deep philosophical waters of death and the afterlife. Like every great work of this kind, it is deceptive in its simplicity. People look at it and say, "Why, that's so simple—I could've done it myself!" And yet, it is incredibly difficult to be simple.

With *Jellybeans*, Sylvia van Ommen has done something incredible. She has given us an uncomplicated and entertaining way to open a discussion with children about life's greatest mystery—death. It is difficult to imagine a treatment of this topic that could leave you smiling, and yet you are holding one now in your hands. George and Oscar—the simple dialogue, the charming line drawings—will survive us all, and deserve our attention as we share books and ideas with the children in our lives.

Jellybeans—oh boy! Any blue ones in there?

Glenn Murray, 2006

jellybeans

Hi. Have you seen how nice it is outside? How about going to the park to eat jellybeans? Bye. Oscar.
P.S. You bring the jellybeans.

O.K. See you later. Bye. George.
P.S. You bring the drinks.

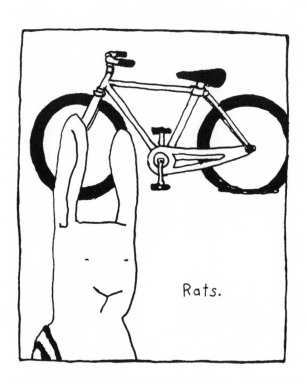

He speeds ahead, leaving his
pursuers far behind. He's
outsmarted them once again.

I'm almost there.   I had a flat tire.

What kind of jellybeans have you got?

A bag of mixed ones.

Hot chocolate.

Great.

I brought some sugar, too.

This one is as blue as the sky.

Do you think . . .

Up there . . .

Do you think there's a heaven up there?

A place you go when you're dead?

I don't know. I think so.

Will we go there, too—
both of us?

I'm going if you're going, that's for sure.

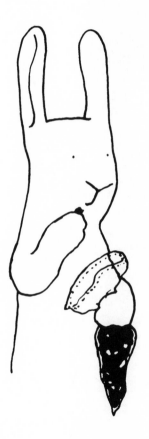

We might bump into
each other there.

That would
be nice.

But what if it's really big and you never bump into anybody?

We can agree to meet at the entrance . . .

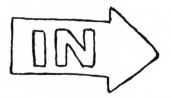

Or at one of those
special meeting places.

Wow, that was fast!   Hey!

But maybe we won't know each other when we get there.

What do you mean?

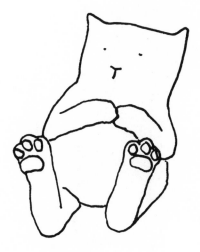

Well, because maybe
when we're dead we
will have forgotten
everything we ever did.

Then there's no sense meeting at the entrance.

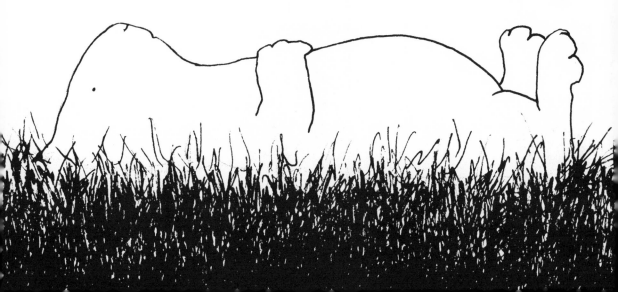

But if we bump into each other
and we don't recognize each other . . .

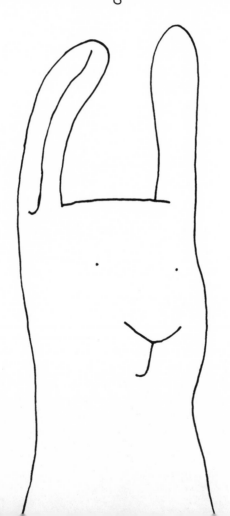

Then we can just become friends all over again.

Eat jellybeans together, stuff like that . . .

Great.

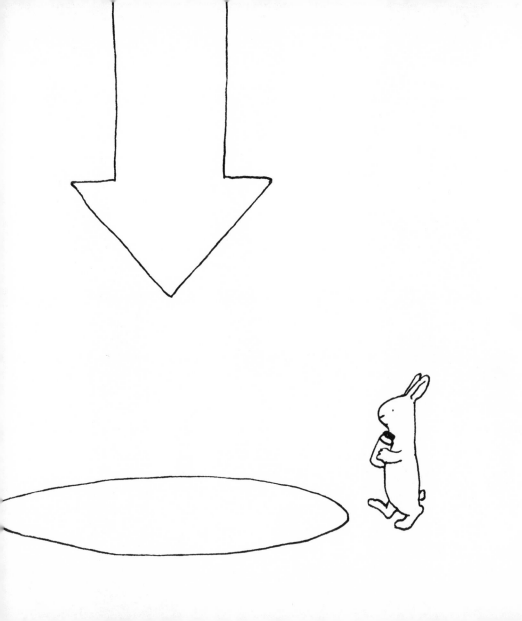

Sylvia van Ommen attended the Academy of Art in Kampen, The Netherlands, and currently lives in Zwolle. *Jellybeans* is the first book she has written and illustrated for children.